D0269567

Maisy's
Library
Card
10-02
1990

First published 2005 by Walker Books Ltd
87 Vauxhall Walk, London SE11 5HJ

2 4 6 8 10 9 7 5 3 1

Illustrated in the style of Lucy Cousins by King Rollo Films Ltd

"Maisy" Audio Visual Series produced by King Rollo Films for Universal Pictures

International Visual Programming

Printed in China

British Library Cataloguing in Publication Data:
a catalogue record for this book is
available from the British Library

ISBN 1-84428-679-7

www.walkerbooks.co.uk

Maisy Goes to the Library

Lucy Cousins

Maisy likes going
to the library.

How lovely to look
at a book in a
nice quiet place.

It was the sort of
day when Maisy wanted
a book about fish.

She found a flappy book
about birds ... but no fish.

She found a shiny green
book about turtles ...

and a great big stripy
book about tigers...
... but no fish!

Never mind,
there are
so many
other things
to do in
the library...

Use the computer...
listen to music...

make a
copy of your
favourite
picture...

look at the
fish in the
aquarium...

Aquarium?

That's it! So Maisy looked by the aquarium...

and that's exactly where
she found a book about fish...
and it was sparkly!

Maisy settled down
to read in a quiet corner.

But then Cyril and Tallulah came along...

and started laughing (at Tallulah's funny face!).

And then Eddie came in...

and shouted "Story time!"

because Ostrich was going to tell a story in the Story corner...

Maisy's quiet corner!

"There was an old woman,
who swallowed
a fly..."

Charley started laughing.

"She swallowed a dog to catch the cat!"

Then everyone started laughing!

Ha-ha-ha!
Meeow!

And they were still laughing when they checked out their books,

and went outside
to play.

In the park, Cyril and Charley pretended to be the old woman and her dog.

Tallulah meowed like a cat... and Eddie neighed like a horse.

Meeeow!

And Maisy...?

Maisy read
her sparkly book
about fish in a
nice . . . *quiet* . . .
place . . .